Early this morning I stumbled out of bed.
I pulled on my jeans and a sweater. It was
drizzling, so I put on a poncho. Then I headed
to the creek.

It had rained enough to make puddles.
My boots squished through the mud. The
day matched my mood perfectly.

I thought about Michael as I walked to
our meeting place. I remembered the day he
had moved into town, three years earlier.
I remembered how different he was from
everyone else I knew. No one could figure
out how we got to be best friends, but we
were. We had been best friends since
second grade.

Gifts

by Jim Fremont
illustrated by Elizabeth Wolf

Scott Foresman

Editorial Offices: Glenview, Illinois • New York, New York
Sales Offices: Reading, Massachusetts • Duluth, Georgia
Glenview, Illinois • Carrollton, Texas • Menlo Park, California

I was working at my computer last night when the phone rang. It was Michael.

"Five o'clock?" he asked.

"Sounds good," I replied. "It might be raining, though."

Michael didn't say anything. I could picture his shrug. Rain never bothered him. It didn't bother me much anymore.

I wanted to say something else, but Michael never liked to talk on the telephone. There wasn't much we could say, anyway.

In the end, all I said was, "See you there."

"Good," he answered.

I'm a good athlete. Because I'm quick and responsible, I'm often a team captain. I like to be surrounded by people, and if I'm not with people, I'm with computers. Since Dad builds and repairs them, working with computers is as natural to me as breathing.

All Michael does is fish.

That's not true. He's a math whiz at school and kids like him. But he really does love to fish most of all. He taught me to love it too.

I tried to teach him to love computers, but I never managed it.

Michael was already fishing when I got to the creek. I watched him reel in his line. He looked as if he really belonged there, with his beat-up hat, his vest, and a knife sheath on his belt.

"I left a rod and reel for you by the rock," he said.

I scrambled over to a boulder by the stream. I picked up the gear and then squished over to the river bank, downstream from Michael.

Michael is a great fly fisherman and he has taught me well. I get more confident with every cast.

There is something special about being outside in the early morning, the steady rushing of the stream, and the rhythmic motions of casting.

Because of Michael, I've learned to think like a fish. Which are the best pools for finding food? Where might an insect float by on the current? Which rocks cast the best shadows for hiding?

I've learned to think like a midge or a grasshopper, drowning in the stream. When I feel enough like a bug and cast my fly just right, a trout surges up and strikes.

Catching a fish always takes my breath away.

Michael taught me to release the fish carefully. That way, there will always be more fish to catch.

We didn't always catch something. This morning, we didn't even feel a nibble. That was OK too.

We fished for about an hour. It was all the time we had left to be with each other. Then I had to get ready to go to school and Michael had to get ready to move.

"Got everything packed?" I asked.
I listened to him reel in his line for the
last time.

Michael nodded. "We'll be driving away
while you're in math class."

"Do you have your fishing list?" I asked
him. I'd downloaded a list from the Internet
of great fishing holes in Maine, where he
was moving.

He reached into a pocket on his fishing
vest and pulled out a folded piece of paper.

"You check them out," I said, "for when
I come to visit."

"I've got something to give you," Michael said, "so you'll remember me. It's at home."

I could have told him I'd never forget him. Every time I visit our fishing stream, I'll be able to picture him casting from his favorite boulder. But I had something for him too. "We'll swing by your house on the way to school," I said.

Michael's house was empty when we got there. His dad's truck was full. So was his mom's car.

Michael handed me a long box. Inside I found a rod, a reel, some flies, a knife in a sheath, and a fishing hat, just like his.

"It won't be the same without you," I said.

"Practice, for when you come to Maine," he said.

Then I gave him a couple of boxes.
Actually, Dad and I shoved them into the
back of his mother's car. His mom had left
just enough space for them. Michael's parents
were in on the surprise.

"I know you don't like computers," I said.
"But Dad and I got a new computer and
thought you could use the old one. This way,
we can keep in touch."

Michael looked at the boxes. He looked at me. "You know what?" he said. "You learned how to cast into a stream and reel in big fish. I ought to be able to cast into the Internet and see what's out there."

"I wrote instructions and my e-mail address," I said. "If you learn to e-mail me, we can talk every day."

Then I went to school.

When I got home at the end of the day, Michael was gone.

Now I'm waiting. I figured it would take him five hours to drive to his new home, three to unpack, one to set up the computer, and one more hour to follow the directions I wrote for him.

So if all goes well, he'll be sending me an e-mail message any minute now.

I hope he sends it soon. Then, first thing tomorrow morning, I'm going fishing.